Al poeta que me dio la
oportunidad de ilustrar una
de las cosas más bellas de este
mundo: el amor entre una
madre y un niño.
A Christina y Adone. — MS

Para mi querida amiga
Anna Uhl Chamot, con
mucho cariño. — JL

To the poet who offered me the
opportunity to illustrate one of
the most beautiful things in this
world: the love between a
mother and a child.
To Christina and Adone. — MS

To my dear friend
Anna Uhl Chamot,
with lots of affection. — JL

OCT 06

Groundwood Books / House of Anansi Press
110 Spadina Avenue, Suite 801,
Toronto, Ontario M5V 2K4
Distribuido en los Estados Unidos por
Publishers Group West
1700 Fourth Street, Berkeley, CA 94710

Library and Archives Canada Cataloguing in
Publication
Luján, Jorge
Tarde de invierno / Jorge Luján; ilustraciones,
Mandana Sadat; traducción, Elisa Amado = Winter
afternoon / by Jorge Luján; pictures by Mandana
Sadat; translated by Elisa Amado.
Text in Spanish and English.
ISBN-13: 978-0-88899-718-0
ISBN-10: 0-88899-718-3
1. Picture books for children. I. Sadat, Mandana
II. Amado, Elisa III. Title.
IV. Title: Winter afternoon.
PZ73.L85Ta 2006   j863'.7   C2005-907453-1

Las ilustraciones fueron realizadas en técnica mixta
y digitalizadas en computadora.

Impreso y encuadernado en China

Groundwood Books / House of Anansi Press
110 Spadina Avenue, Suite 801,
Toronto, Ontario M5V 2K4
Distributed in the USA by Publishers Group West
1700 Fourth Street, Berkeley, CA 94710

Library and Archives Canada Cataloguing in
Publication
Luján, Jorge
Tarde de invierno / Jorge Luján; ilustraciones,
Mandana Sadat; traducción, Elisa Amado = Winter
afternoon / by Jorge Luján; pictures by Mandana
Sadat; translated by Elisa Amado.
Text in Spanish and English.
ISBN-13: 978-0-88899-718-0
ISBN-10: 0-88899-718-3
1. Picture books for children. I. Sadat, Mandana
II. Amado, Elisa III. Title.
IV. Title: Winter afternoon.
PZ73.L85Ta 2006   j863'.7   C2005-907453-1

The illustrations are in mixed media, scanned and
composed on computer.

Printed and bound in China

Tarde de invierno
Winter Afternoon

Jorge Luján

ilustraciones / pictures by **Mandana Sadat**

traducción / translated by Elisa Amado

Libros Tigrillo

Groundwood Books / House of Anansi Press

Toronto   Berkeley

Juega mi dedo en el
vidrio empañado

My finger plays on
the frosty glass.

y dibuja una luna

I have drawn a moon.

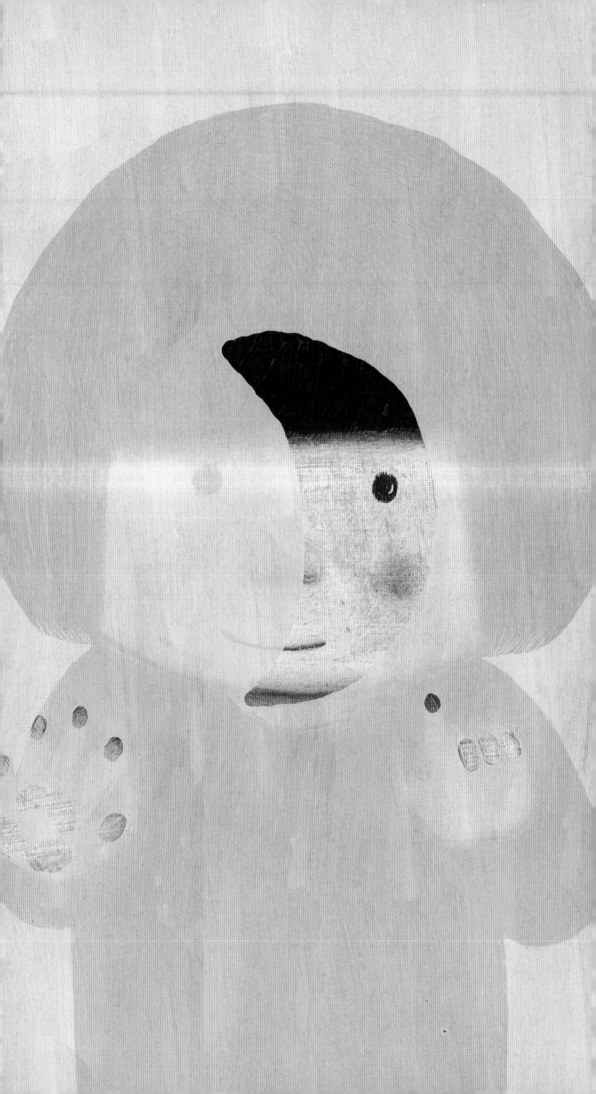

y dentro de ella a mi madre

Inside the moon my mother

que viene por la calle

is walking
down the street.

y cabe justo en el dibujo

She fits just so and I make my picture

que voy agrandando a medida que
se va acercando

bigger as she comes closer

hasta darme este abrazo

until she is giving me a hug

que cabe exactamente

that fits exactly

detrás del vidrio del portarretrato.

into the frosty frame.